On Wimbledon Common, under the ground in their Burrow, live

The **W**OMBLES

Orinoco the Magnificent

Adapted by Elisabeth Beresford

from the Wombles television series produced by CINAR and UFTP

Hodder
Children's
Books

a division of Hodder Headline plc

One morning, a sleepy Orinoco was tidying up the Common. There was a strange noise in the distance. But Orinoco didn't notice anything until he almost tripped over an old box. Inside was a magician's hat, a cape and a wand.

"It's a magic set!" said Orinoco. He put on the hat, closed his eyes and waved the wand. "Abracadabra!" he said. "Please get rid of all this rubbish!"

And at that moment, a whirlwind shot by with a 'whoosh', and dropped all the rubbish into Orinoco's tidy bag.

Orinoco opened his eyes and saw the full tidy bag.

"I'm magic!" he shouted. "I'm Orinoco the Magnificent!"

Inside the Burrow, Tobermory had just had a message from the Wombles in the Thames Burrow.

"It says that they are sending us one of their young Wombles called Stepney. They want him to find out how much rubbish we clear up on the Common. It says that he's a 'Whizz Womble'!"

In the kitchen, Madame Cholet was busy making bramble cakes. Orinoco hurried in to tell her about his new magic powers.

"I can do magic now," said Orinoco. "I can make rubbish vanish . . ."

"Please vanish from my kitchen," said Madame Cholet. "I am very, very busy!"

"Yes, Madame Cholet," said Orinoco and he did vanish, with some of her cakes. He was just eating the last crumbs when Tomsk and Bungo came hurrying up.

"Guess what," said Bungo, "our tidy bags have magically filled themselves with rubbish!"

"My powers must be stronger than I thought!" exclaimed Orinoco. "It's me! I did it. I'm Orinoco the Magnificent!"

But nobody believed him. They just laughed.

The next day Alderney and Shansi were flying over the Common in the Womcopter. They were looking out for rubbish and really enjoying themselves.

"What's that?" said Alderney, looking down.

"It looks like a whirlwind!"

Far, far below them Stepney was whirling across the Common with his wheeliebarrow. This was his machine for picking up rubbish, and it was very fast indeed – fast enough to make a whirlwind when it passed by!

"I'm Stepney Womble. And I've come to show you how we tidy up in our Thames Burrow."

"If you think your Burrow is better than ours, let's have a competition to see who can collect the most rubbish!" said Alderney, who was really quite cross.

Of course, all the Wombles lined up
for the start of the race, with Orinoco
holding the stopwatch.
"One, two, three . . . GO!"

Away went Stepney with his wheeliebarrow and Alderney was just picking up an old umbrella when he whizzed past, taking the brolly with him, and she sat down with a thump.

Orinoco was waving his magic wand, but it didn't seem to be working because his tidy bag stayed empty. And at the end of the race, although the Wimbledon Wombles had worked very hard, Stepney had tidied up the most rubbish, so he'd won!

However, Wellington had just had one of his great ideas and off he went to the Workshop with Alderney. He was going to invent a tidying-up machine himself.

The machine was a skootboard and as soon as it was finished they
went to try it out.

The very next day Bungo, Tomsk and Orinoco were all lined up
ready to start work when they heard a strange noise, a sort of VROOM
VROOM, and straight towards them came Alderney and Wellington on
the skootboard.

"This'll show Stepney how fast *we* can work," said Alderney. "Please give me my tidy bag, Orinoco, and off we go. VROOM VROOM!"

Stepney had been working so hard that he thought he'd just have a little sleep before he got back to the Burrow, and he never heard Alderney come riding past.

Alderney scooped up all his rubbish and off she went. Stepney couldn't believe his eyes when he woke up and saw that his wheeliebarrow was empty. Very slowly he walked back to the Burrow.

"Never mind, young Womble," said Tobermory, "the others have just been playing a bit of a joke on you. Now then, let's start as friends all over again! Come in and have your supper."

Everybody laughed and clapped when Stepney walked into the kitchen and soon he began to laugh too. Especially when Orinoco said, "Now then - who wants to see *my* magic trick? It's called 'making your supper disappear!' VROOM VROOM!"

Photographs and original artwork,
courtesy of FilmFair Ltd.
a subsidiary of CINAR Films Inc.

ISBN 0 340 735805

10 9 8 7 6 5 4 3 2 1

A catalogue record for this book
is available from the British Library.
The right of Elisabeth Beresford to be identified as the
author of this work has been asserted by her.

Printed in Great Britain

Hodder Children's Books
a division of Hodder Headline plc
338 Euston Road, London NW1 3BH